slipper

dreams,

shattered

doungjai**gam**

published by apokrupha

cover by robert ford, whutta.com

isbn: 978-1721770724

copyright 2018

apokrupha.com

advanced praise for
glass slipper dreams, shattered

Gam delivers devastating punches in this collection of short-shorts, taking our breath away with a turn of a phrase, a dark play on words; every syllable paints unexpected shadows in our imagination.

—Linda D. Addison, award-winning author of *How to Recognize a Demon Has Become Your Friend* and HWA Lifetime Achievement Award winner

Reminiscent of Mercedes Yardley's work, Doungjai Gam's stories and prose poems are small gems filled with heartbreak, sorrow, and longing, but they also hold light in the darkness and hope in the despair. Lovely!

—Damien Angelica Walters, author of *Cry Your Way Home*

Tales brimming with fear, dread and horror—a strong, unique new voice!

—Thomas Tessier, author of *Phantom*

doungjai gam writes powerful vignettes, songs of darkness and sorrow, anger and pain, with a beautiful prose style. Each tale, regardless of length, another examination of the human condition and the fragments left behind when a soul is shattered. Beautifully tragic.

—James A. Moore, author of the Serenity Falls Trilogy

doungjai gam's flash fiction exists in a liminal space between poetry and assassination. Every single word in *Glass Slipper Dreams, Shattered* was chosen for its greatest impact, and the stories are all breathtakingly precise and perfectly honed. Slow down and take your time with these stories. Gam's beautiful writing is so sharp it could cut a shadow.

—Bracken MacLeod, author of *Come To Dust* and *13 Views Of The Suicide Woods*

for these brothers three,

who've enriched my life dearly

with friendship and laughter

and so much love

...you are all missed.

Dave Piscitelli

1978-2015

Eddie Bepko

1978-2016

Tommy Dow

1962-2016

glass
slipper
dreams,
shattered

I'll make you famous

She approached me at the bar, drunk and needing someone, anyone. Her name was Pam or Sam Something. Another starlet wannabe who couldn't land a role. Buxom figure, average face, a touch naïve.

We shared a bottle of bourbon, and then went for a drive. I helped her stagger into a storage unit I rented. She belched and giggled while I set up the camcorder and hit the 'record' button.

"Is this an audition?"

I pulled a knife out of a nearby duffel bag and turned to her.

"You could say that..."

best served warm

Take peanuts—one for every "late night" he worked, two for every time you kissed him and tasted her lingering on his lips—and grind them into bits. Mix them into his favorite Thai takeout, which you picked up earlier. Reheat, then add a squirt of Sriracha for good measure. Serve it with a smile when he's fresh out of the shower. Sit with him, even though you already ate.

Hide the EpiPens. Relish the moment.

huntress

Although killing brings Sasha much exultant joy, she prefers the hunt. It's in her tenacious nature to lay waiting for the precise moment to strike. But for now she's content to sunbathe on the deck, the warmth engulfing her.

And then he shows up.

"Sasha, bad girl!" He points at her offering to him. It's a masterpiece; she's never caught a woodpecker before and she's proud of this.

He tries to kick her, but she moves quickly. She's still sore from the last time.

She hisses at him. While he sleeps, she'll create a new masterpiece using her claws and his throat.

lake of secrets

Ah, we meet again.

I knew you'd come back. I'm not a whorish gossip, like the wind or the trees. I am here, steadfast and trustworthy. I look calm on the surface, but what hides beneath would challenge anyone's sanity.

But you know this—after all, you've never come to me in the middle of the night with pretensions of innocence. So give me your offerings. Give me your secrets, your fears.

Until next time, I promise you this:

I will not give up your secrets.

I will not give up your dead.

love. lust. obsession. whatever.

I loved you.

You loved her and lusted me. For a while, that was okay. Like a stupid girl with glass slipper dreams, I did everything you wanted with the hopes that one day, you would love me back. The weight of the torch I carried crippled me.

But now you're mine, and every cut I inflict upon you will sting like it did whenever you said her name to me. Before I reach in to yank your heart out, I lean down and whisper one last sweet nothing:

"If I can't have a happily ever after, you don't get one either."

evening theft

He whispers: *What am I still to you?*

Everywhere I turn, you're there. The shaggy haired young man standing at the corner. The street musician strumming his guitar. You've even permeated my dreams, smiling as you reach for me.

The man on the corner turns, and he's not you. The musician can't hit the same notes you can. As for the dreams...well, I wake up alone.

What are you still? You know you're everything to me. Time refuses to heal my wounds.

Damn it, why did you go swimming in the marina that night? Why did you leave me behind?

swallowed in pieces, consumed in whole

I gouged out my eyeballs in order to not look at you. I swallowed my tongue so you couldn't touch it with yours. I bit, scratched, and maimed the parts of me you hadn't ruined yet so that you would stay away.

You still conquered, reveling in my self harm. Your unhinged serpentine mouth took me in, a feast battered down just enough to be consumed whole, but I refused to acquiesce to your bloodthirsty desires. With ragged fingernails, I clawed at your innards until you expel me from your belly.

Bloody and mutilated, I staggered away while you lay dying.

christmas lights in february

(suicidal rumination #1)

February, unseasonably mild. The seatbelt's unbuckled and the convertible top down because it stopped raining.

You've been down this road before—all dark and narrow with sharp curves—but that was long ago. On nights like this when all is wrong, there is comfort in being here and taking those curves a little too fast.

In the distance, many rays of hope twinkle. You're drawn to them like sailors to the Sirens, with a similar ending. Hurled from the crash, you soar over the mist-covered lake and for a brief moment, you feel the sweet freedom that has always eluded you.

one day we will dance again

"Do you like my gown?" Barefoot in a blue slipdress, she radiates elegance. When I bow to her, she giggles and grabs my hands. We dance in slow lazy circles, the full moon our spotlight. "My prom queen," I murmur in her ear. The song she softly hums is cut off by blaring in the distance, growing louder.

"I hear the sirens." She backs away, covered in blood—is it hers? Mine?

Then I remember the crash.

"We have to go." She tugs on me and we run from the wreck, from our broken corpses, and towards the next life.

the eater of dreams

There's something about him you're attracted to, but you can't quite place it. His looks are average, but he's polite and friendly, and sometimes that's enough.

You enjoy each other's company; things get intimate fast. Late night, limbs tangled in bedsheets. He nervously fumbles with your jeans, so eager to get in. His fingers are close, his lips near yours. And—

Sunlight. Reality.

Fuck.

You dread seeing him at work. When he smiles and says hi, you try not to blush. You think of the dream and curse the sun for denying you the sweet ending.

torn

Anne wakes up in pieces; the night before just a vague recollection. *This needs to stop*, she thinks. She tries to sigh but exhales through her nose instead. Sitting up, she discovers that her lips and both legs are gone.

Not again.

She drags herself around the house, looking for her missing pieces. Her legs and feet are separated; she remembers this time to tuck the nerves back in. She licks her dry lips after reattaching them.

She paces the floor with wobbly legs, but that feeling will pass. With whole body and sound mind, she reminds herself to never let a guy get so close to her that he can wreck her like that again.

noises, magnified by silence

When you awaken at 3am, the sound of your eyelashes brushing against the comforter could be mistaken for the rustling of a pant leg of someone walking too close to the bed. Floorboards creak as the house settles…or maybe an intruder as he tiptoes on that loose step.

Though your heart beats so hard it threatens to break your ribcage, you chide yourself for reading those silly horror stories before bed.

Breathe in.

Breathe out.

Slowly.

Quietly.

Before long, slumber pulls you in. While you sleep, you never see the shadow it as moves from the corner, reaching for you.

repose

And for a moment it seems easy to give in, to allow the gnarled fingers of darkness to shut your eyelids and guide you into the unknown. You hear its rasping voice – *"No one will miss you when you're gone"* – and you almost believe.

You wait for the light, with its promises of healing and tranquility, but it eludes you. You wonder—how much longer?

And then—a dazzling radiance, warming you like summer's embrace. Calm settles over your being.

You've lived to survive another night, but still you wonder: for how much longer?

the south rises again

The weather predictions were wrong. Again.

The three feet of snow that was expected fell within hours. What panicked everyone was that it continued for weeks. Power lines went down, roofs caved in. The entire North was frozen and eerily quiet—a Western Siberia.

The South, long resentful of their neighbors, rejoiced in the streets while hoisting their maligned flags. Life was good until the heat wave.

The waters rose quickly, and the Mississippi and the Rio Grande refused to be ignored. Dams burst, flooding the lands. The North and South were reunited again under a blanket of water and destruction.

the key is the key

It's in there somewhere, he knows it is. He can feel It bouncing and rolling around on a distracted elliptical orbit, just out of reach.

He slaps his forehead in frustration—*think!* The sudden jolt forces It to change direction, sliding backwards off the trail and further into the unknown.

Damn it, another thought gone. Once on the tip of his tongue, now trapped in the ever-growing wasteland of his brain. The doctor said it would happen quick—

He stares at the house keys in his hand, trying to recall what they are and what they're used for.

rebirth

Light surges through me and energizes my core. I stand at full height, leaving my dormancy behind for another season. My body leans toward the sun as my roots dig deeper into the dirt. My hairs are full and blond, but one day they will gray and fall away, spreading my seed everywhere. Go on and behead me, pluck me from the ground—I will keep coming back, ravenous and intent on domination. Only when the air turns cold and darkness threatens to take over the day is when I go back into hiding, plotting my next takeover.

mama's wrath

Mama's angry again.

She gets this way every summer. I think it's a combination of the heat and the sudden onset of ill-mannered vacationers. She hates their unruliness and destructive tendencies.

Her eyes darken as we watch them dirty the landscape—detritus on the streets, broken bottles on the beach.

"Enough!" she screams.

Her inhalation is deep, and she exhales hurricanes and tidal waves. There's death and downed trees, people carried out to sea.

When she sees what she's done, she cries. She always cries.

"When will they learn?" she says softly.

in his dreams...

(for Dave)

...he isn't tethered to wires so he floats like a stray feather on a vernal breeze. Anger, disease, suffering—none of these exist here. Peace and warmth envelop him, the feelings growing stronger the longer he sleeps

...until angry voices awaken him. Foreign hands prod and jab him. Pain—his ever-present companion—races through his being. The drugs kick in quickly

...and he's at a familiar wooded path strewn with debris and anguish. With unsteady feet, he walks toward the clearing ahead and sits at his favorite rock so he can watch the sunrise. The morning light embraces him as he smiles and slowly disappears.

...in the realm beyond dreams, youth is eternal and pain is but a notion.

mourninglight

It should be dawn, but the sun never came up. People stared at their timepieces in confusion and listened for birds that had stopped chirping. Scientists and weathermen failed in their quests for answers.

After the generators died, people fought and killed for the last of the batteries. Once those were depleted in both quantity and power, insanity set in. Family members killed their own, mistaking them for intruders. Street corner poets lamented the lack of color, of structure, of anything.

Then one day there was a pinprick of light in the darkness, a little dot that quickly tore the sky open. Those who survived the darkness were obliterated as the heat melted their flesh. The oceans boiled over and evaporated. Carcasses—human and animal alike—littered the land and stank up the atmosphere as the sun charred the earth's surface. The last of the planet's ashes hadn't begun to dissipate before the sun moved on to its next victim.

...and now I can move on.

Let me out. His roars are thunderous. *No way in hell,* you think. He's a poisonous distraction, one best kept locked up. But you feel terrible, so you crack the door open. He swoops out, an intense thunderstorm intent on destruction. You fight and embrace, you love and you hate. Battered down, you finally secure him away again. He pounds on the door and screams. In time it becomes easier to ignore him.

When all goes quiet, you check on him to find that the storm that flooded your life is now merely a puddle, shallow and defeated.

footsteps.

(for Eddie)

I know you're there...

You're pacing the hallway in your combat boots, looking for a fight...running down the basketball court in your favorite pair of beat up sneakers, nailing that jump shot...rounding the bases in your cleats, jumping and stomping on home plate, thrilled about your first home run.

I hear you now on the stone path, loose bits of rocks crunching under your shoes. The bench groans from the pressure as you sit down next to me.

I turn to you.

You're not there, but I know you are and always will be.

light box

The light box instructions say that the bulbs burn out faster with constant usage. But its powers are healing, especially when winter's dreariness seeps into my mind and whispers of terrible deeds I should perform.

Two hours of staring at this light, yet darkness holds tight to my soul.

Last night, the neighbor's dog wouldn't stop yapping. Something had to be done. Now their kid's outside crying, searching for a dog he'll never find.

The light box flickers. Darkness seduces me again. *The boy*, it says. *Take him out.*

It's only January. I'm going to need more light bulbs.

beware of darkness

It sidles up to you, wrapping around you with false promises of warmth. And it feels wonderful at first, until its tendrils snake their way into your mind and twist every last thought into paranoia and hatred, all the while reassuring you that you've done no wrong. Comfort becomes a soft yet warm pillow you can't turn over.

Then: light, brash in its appearance, resistant to your tears, insistent that you work and not be coddled. It promises happiness, but a long winding road to travel.

Genuine warmth versus ignorance of light.

Which one do you choose?

bloodrain

Helena sobbed in the shower as she scrubbed everywhere her husband touched her. The hot water calmed her, yet the bruises remained. Before bed, she prayed to the goddess for peace and strength.

She awoke the next morning alone to a bloodstorm thundering. For five days and five nights, red rain poured down thick and heavy. Cultists called for the end of times. Others were afraid and stayed inside.

But the battered and bullied knew, and they rejoiced in the streets. Children splashed in crimson puddles, knowing that those who hurt them were now gone. Though waking up alone was typical, she knew something was different this time. She stepped out of her house and as the blood rained down on her, she felt the fear and lack of self-esteem melt away. She thanked the goddess and embraced her new self.

Naked and free, Helena danced in the rain.

candy apple

Mrs J's candy apples were usually popular, but no children went to her house on Halloween. Rumor had it she wanted to poison the kids who had bullied her preteen daughter Beth into committing suicide.

Jenna had been Beth's only friend. She stopped at Mrs J's house a week after the funeral. After some awkward chat, she accepted a candy apple. Because she skipped lunch earlier that day, she devoured the treat quickly.

When Jenna was ready to leave, she tried to stand but fell over in pain. She clutched her stomach and groaned.

Mrs J's voice was cold: "You were her only friend. Why didn't you stand up for her?"

reflection

(suicidal rumination #2)

I know she's me, but I don't recognize her.

She's the 'me' I used to be—slender, with long thick curls and a light sprinkling of freckles—a happy girl. We stare at each other, not talking. Then she smiles at me.

I remember when I used to smile.

I reach out to her but as I move closer to the surface I think twice about it and begin to pull away. Her hand continues to come forward and she breaks the surface to grab me. Her grip is seductive, even as she drags my wrist over a jagged piece of mirror. Her eyes and smile—*my* eyes and smile—remind me of what was and what can be.

I stop fighting and let her take me.

the dying house

Whenever Anna thought of her childhood home, her head throbbed. Most thought it was the stress from the knowledge of her entire family dying at the homestead, all at different times from causes both natural and sudden. Those close to her knew better; they could see the ghost behind her eyes begging to be set free.

The urge to return home grew stronger and she relented one day. Her headaches screamed as she walked around the house, but they slowly dissipated as she entered her childhood bedroom. She lay on her old bed. For a moment, calm enveloped her.

Then the pain began anew. She pressed the heels of her palms against her eyes to make it stop and panicked when her eyes bled. She screamed in agony as her eyes hemorrhaged. When Anna went quiet, her ghost rose from the bloody wreckage of her face and left the room in silence, seeking out the others.

that girl with the hair

She sat alone at the bar sipping a colorful drink when he approached with whiskey bravado. She stared at him coolly with one eye, the other hidden underneath a brunette wave. She rejected his advances and excused herself to use the ladies' room. He knew this trick, and quietly trailed her as she slipped out the side door. Before she left the alley, he grabbed her shoulder and whirled her around.

"Going somewhere?" He yanked her hair.

"No—please don't," she begged. He laughed as he pulled her closer and brushed her hair back to reveal her hidden eye.

"What the hell—?"

Moments later, she smiled as she fixed her hair, covering her right eye which, when covered, no longer glowed.

Another man turned into stone. With one touch he turned into rubble.

"I warned you."

some animals eat their young

Robby's still alive. *Now* is the time to panic.

Elaine sits behind the wheel and tries to gather her scattering thoughts. That hit should have taken him out, but here he is rolling onto his side. She wonders if she should dare a second try.

She's sure none of this is happening the way it should be—she shouldn't have discovered him mutilating the body of a local missing girl in the shed. He shouldn't have chased her. She shouldn't have tried to kill him.

He struggles to stand. His eyes are full of hatred. Any last traces of her son are now gone.

He takes a pained step towards her. Elaine hits the gas.

waste not, want not

"...and the rest of her?"

"Save the bones for stock, the fat for soap. The skin can be tanned and made into leather."

"Gertrude..."

"Not another word, John." She pounded her fist on the table where the corpse of their son's wife lay. He knew better than to say another word.

"She cheated—*you saw it*. She deserves to be chewed up and shat out by the ones she betrayed."

Outside, a car approached. Gertrude gestured to John.

"Freeze her." She went upstairs to greet her son and kids.

"My darlings, I've made lasagna with homemade sausage for dinner!"

alone in the hall

It's just a hallway.

Ignore the shadows thrown on the walls by piss-colored lighting. Ignore the scuttling noises in the walls made by small creatures that are stuck and are likely to end up rotting in there. Ignore those who are lurking in the dark corners, whispering threats they claim they will act on if you walk by them without a word.

It's just a hallway.

The faces you see and walk by every day—familiar and strange alike—it's hard to say which ones you can trust and which ones would shove you down the stairwell. Which one of them would follow you into the public bathroom and attack you. Which one of them would smile at you, or sneer as if you were a dirt smudge on a white dress.

It's just a hallway.

Take one step, and another, and another. Find your rhythm. Pay no mind to the soft echo of footsteps behind you and the sigh of the blade being released from its sheath.

It's just a hallway.

dead weight

Andrew came home one night and found what was left of Lisa on the bed.

Once upon a time, she had been a loving and affectionate partner. As the years passed, her passion ebbed and they fought frequently. Her kisses were perfunctory; sex became a chore. The words "I love you" were difficult to say, like phlegm you can't dislodge no matter how hard you cough.

One day she began to itch. As their quarrels worsened, so did her symptoms. The doctors and specialists were baffled, the medicines useless. She clawed herself in her sleep and cried in the morning when she saw dried blood on the bed sheets and ragged fingernail trails on her limbs and torso.

Before long Lisa was cutting everyone out of her life. She quit her job and shut down her social media accounts. After that she locked herself in the spare bedroom and refused to come out for anybody, even Andrew. The one time she did open the door to him, he was horrified at the sight of her. Her skin was red and raw, the open sores encrusted with blood. Scaly patches of skin littered the floor. She refused to make eye contact with him.

For better or for worse, he reminded himself.

And then he came home to this...this *husk* lying on her side of the bed. He brushed it with the tip of his finger, afraid that it would break.

It was harder than he had expected, rougher than a shod snakeskin.

Andrew didn't bother with eating or going online that night. After sitting on the edge of the bed and crying for over an hour, he got into his pajamas and lay next to the shell of his wife. He sobbed and moaned, eventually succumbing to a nightmare-fueled slumber, filled with tossing, turning, and the hope that when he awoke the next morning he would discover this to be nothing more than a bad dream he would not inflict on anyone.

He awoke at daybreak and was dismayed to find it still there. He called in sick to work and stayed in bed for the remainder of the workweek and the weekend. Eating and housekeeping no longer mattered. After the third day he unplugged the answering machine and took the phone off the hook.

When the husk wilted, he burned it in the fire pit. The gray smoke undulated seductively against the night sky—another reminder of Lisa and the woman she used to be.

When the fire was put out, when the mourning was over for the last time, he went to the spare bedroom where she spent her final days. He sat on the floor and waited. Silence and guilt hung heavy in the air, permeating his flesh. A terrible itching sensation came over him and he clawed at his arms and torso.

He wondered who would find him.

cold

It's knee-deep in winter on the Connecticut shore and the few beach houses on this cul-de-sac aren't in use right now. There are no streetlamps along the road, and the light reflecting off the crescent moon makes a dull impression on the snow-mottled ground. I lean against the side of a small house that has seen better days and peek around the corner. The houses are dark, the driveways unoccupied.

There's no one here to see me, and that is exactly what I want.

I scurry through backyards and come to a halt when I see the beach house of my childhood. Using the key I swiped from my dad, I let myself in the back door and grimace at the musty smell when I step inside. I fish around in my backpack and find my flashlight, but its batteries are old, the light too dim. I leave it on the kitchen table; knowing my parents and their reluctance to change anything, I should be able to make my way around the house on memory alone.

Relics from the past offer me comfort as I walk through the house. The fleece blanket folded neatly over the threadbare couch reminds me of the chilly summer nights when, as a kid, my mom and I would sit on the deck, wrapped up together for warmth as we watched the tides go out. Near the staircase is a small hutch of figurines my mom collected over the years. I reach in and run my hand over a particular piece that has a slender and shapely form. When I reach the figure's neckline, I feel the glue that keeps her head attached to her body.

Inside me, a familiar anger rises.

Step away. I've already failed once tonight to suppress my rage.

I need to get upstairs, because I don't have much time left. I take the stairs one by one, making sure to skip the tenth one with the creaky board that my father never bothered to replace. In complete darkness now, I count the paces to my bedroom—*one two three* watch out for the table by the bathroom door, *eleven twelve thirteen* there's the doorknob. My hand lingers on it for a moment before I swing the door open and find that—much like the rest of the house—nothing has changed.

Interesting how there's comfort in stagnancy.

I glance at every corner of the room, a mild panic ready to burst wide open. I spot the item I'm looking for: the conch shell I found on the beach when I was eleven. Holding it again for the first time in years, the memories rush over me: the excitement of finding a near-intact shell larger than my hand and the way my mom held it with reverence as she gave it a thorough exam to make sure it wasn't inhabited. My fingers run over the surface, mostly smooth with the occasional hole or crack that no doubt hold secret stories of what it's like to live in the ocean.

And then, a new sensation—a hard, ragged line that feels like the same glue used to keep my mother's figurine together. One tear, followed by another starts a deluge as more memories rush to the surface for air. The sadness in my mom's voice as she reminds me that

I'm a good boy. The way she spent most of her summers in scarves and sunglasses. It wasn't to look fashionable; she had to be creative to cover up my father's handiwork. In my case he liked to aim for my legs, usually the upper thighs so my swim trunks could cover the bruises.

For a moment, my grip tightens on the shell as I glare out the window. At the end of the road, a car drives by slowly. Too slowly. My heart sinks as I see the headlights become brighter as the car turns onto this road.

My time is up, but they're not going to catch me. I race down the stairs and into the kitchen. I place the shell next to the flashlight. I pull a note from my pocket and leave it unfolded on the table. One last time I rummage through my backpack and find my father's gun, which I place on top of the note. I leave through the back door and run across the beach. I'm calf-deep in the water by the time the police have parked. It's so fucking cold but I keep going. Behind me, voices yell for me to come out of the water. In my head, voices echo in cacophony: my mom crying as she was beat by someone she trusted, my father bellowing that I would never amount to anything, my own screams as a frightened child. The one I hear the loudest is also the one that is the quietest...my mother telling me that she loved me more than anything in the world. They were the last words she spoke to me before her "accidental" fall down the stairs into the basement. I still wonder if I could have saved her if I hadn't gone out that night.

My body is numb but my face is hot with tears. Waves slosh at my chest and neck. In my mind, I keep seeing my father dead in his bed by my hand and his gun. I try to think instead of warm days, of the shell I forgot to bring with me so it could go home again. As the waves push harder, insistent that I join them, I mutter the words written on the note left behind:

"I did this for my mother. This was not self-defense."

in the garden

Melinda's final wish was to have her ashes scattered across the gardens in the backyard of the home she and Darren bought almost two decades earlier. Even as her health worsened, she devoted as much time as she was able to cultivating her fruits and flowers. In her final days, the blooms began to wilt as if mourning, despite a sufficient rainfall that should have made up for the lack of watering.

A month after her death, on what would have been their twenty-fifth anniversary, Darren carried out Melinda's request and sprinkled some of her ashes in the flower beds and at the bases of the raspberry bushes. He poured a healthy portion around her rose bush. She had spent many an hour lavishing care and attention to her roses.

Ashes to ashes and all that; now she was reunited with her favorite plant.

In moments of sadness he would walk through the gardens to feel closer to her spirit, but there was never any moment where he felt something that he would call a sign. The chimes never clanged on a windless day. The flowers didn't bloom in a clandestine pattern that only he could decipher as a message from beyond. And the cardinals—Melinda's favorite bird, the one she referred to as a 'ghost bird' because when she felt sad about losing her mother, a cardinal would show up—they stopped coming around.

It took some years, but one day he felt ready to move on. He met

Amy through a friend. She had been divorced for years and had made it clear that she wasn't looking for a romance, but their first meet-up for coffee turned into a daylong walk around town followed by dinner. From there the relationship blossomed quickly and it wasn't long before she moved in with him. There were many evenings in the autumn they would walk through the backyard and he would show off the years of hard work Melinda had put into the gardens. Amy had a mild interest at best, but when spring rolled around she declined his invitations to walk around outside. High pollen counts and a severe allergy to bee stings, she said. Hurt, he tried to shrug it off and walk alone. On more than one occasion he would look back at the house and catch her staring at the rose bush with disdain.

 Summertime came, and Darren spent more time with the rose bush, trimming it back and trying to avoid the bees. In the years since Melinda passed, the bush continued to grow and he found that it needed more attention than he had first realized. A mourning dove cooed nearby and he turned to look for it. In his haste, he scraped his forearm against several thorns. He cursed and wiped the blood using the front of his t-shirt.

 As he stood up, a tightness in his chest caused him to double over. Amy, watching from the comfort of the kitchen, rushed outside to help him lay down. She flailed in anger at the branches of the rose bush that seemed to come close to her. She tried to channel her anger into punching Darren's chest, hoping that would somehow revive him. It didn't work.

As Amy cried, a branch heavy with thorns snaked around her throat and pulled her against the bush. Smaller branches just as thorny curled around her limbs and dug in. She cried out and struggled to break free, but they gripped her tighter. Her eyes widened with desperation as she saw the bees approaching. The swarm overtook her, and once her final breath was taken it almost seemed as if the bush shoved her to the ground.

A pair of thick branches reached out to Darren and wound themselves under his arms and across his torso. He was dragged gently to the bush, where he was embraced and caressed by so many wooden arms. As the sun went down, the bush began to feed.

timekeeper

(for Tommy)

We keep time by counting down the minutes. We watch the second hand tick at a steady beat as we anxiously await the end of a school day or a conference call that seems endless. Meanwhile, the hour and minute hands keep their respective rhythms.

We time our steps to the beat of a drum. Three-fourths time, seven-eighths time—it all depends on who's manning the drum kit. While we march to our own beat, we oftentimes find ourselves drawn to the cadence of another and we abandon our rhythm for their frenetic pace.

Then through some sort of human error or something out of our control, the beat gets lost. The drumstick misses the cymbal, the foot slips off the bass pedal. Cacophony descends and the once-reliant timekeeper struggles to find the beat again.

We all keep time in different measures. Whereas before we counted the minutes, we now count the pills that must be administered at certain times of the day. We can count the number of songs we listen to on our commute, or we can mark the days on the calendar with thick black X's—in the end, it's another day survived. We count seconds, hours, breaths—anything to remind us we are still here amongst the living.

And when we're gone, the ones we leave behind revert back to their own beats in whatever fashion suits them—all to remind themselves that the clock is still there, watching and waiting to claim our beat.

    ticktock

    tick tock

    tick tock

       tick

          tock

            ...tick

how you killed me.

it starts innocently enough—

a tendon that calcifies,

then nausea hits:

a black roiling smog

rendering my insides numb

with every rejection,

ossification spreads

through muscles and organs,

saturating the dermis

as I slowly asphyxiate

I reach into myself

to give you my final offering

you drop it,

stomp on it—

a pulpy mess

with bloody bits stuck to your boot

my stone flesh crumbles

as tears flow like rain

limbs shatter

as they hit the floor

and you:

the sole witness to my destruction,

can't even be bothered to pick up

the broken pieces of me

before you walk away

to start anew.

what remains

It's that same nightmare again, isn't it?

You know, the one where you and your brother are sleeping at your grandmother's house and you hear something at the door. When he goes to investigate he finds the handle on the screen door missing and shadows lurking outside. He tells you to call 911, but when you pick up your grandmother's phone—you remember, the beige rotary with the long cord—you find the line dead. Your brother screams from the doorway. You feel dread beginning to suffocate you, and—

This is the point where you wake up, your heart pumping hot terror through your veins. You think you're awake—you're *sure* you're awake—but you see the nightmare continue on in your mind's eye. And what you see is that you're a kid again, cowering under your blankets.

What are you doing?

Get out from under those blankets—you are not a child anymore, and all the pretending in the world will not turn your comforter into an invisibility cloak. You thought that if you hid, the Reaper would float by unawares and continue to search elsewhere for the next victim. Oh, how you cried every night of your childhood, afraid of death and darkness as you slept under layers of blankets through weather hot and cold. Your parents would find you in the morning drenched by the sweat that fled your pores the previous night.

But that was then, and so on. And you're still hiding.

From the stairs you hear a long, low *creeeaaak*, and whatever wisps of sleepiness that were lingering have now left you completely. When the noise stops, so does your heart—but only for a moment. You relax a bit when you hear the patter of four little paws trotting across the carpet, then the eventual meow as Patches jumps on the bed. Her purrs are content as her claws pierce the fabric of the comforter. She kneads for what seems like several minutes before she curls up at your feet. The weight and warmth of her soothe your nerves. Everything seems okay until you shift to your right side. A soft thump on the floor and you know she's gone.

Yet the weight remains.

Your body goes rigid while your heart hurls itself repeatedly against your ribcage. You try to be subtle as you curl deeper into yourself, but the mattress groans against your movements. You find yourself wishing that someone was here to comfort you, but who? You're all alone here, even though you are one of many in this massive apartment building, which is merely one of thousands that stand in a city that doesn't know slumber.

Sad, isn't it...how loneliness can pervade your soul even while you're surrounded by so many.

And now here you are—alone, quivering in fear—left to wonder what remains at the foot of your bed. What is it? Neither heavy nor light, neither warm nor cold...it's just *there*.

Why don't you sit up and take a look?

thy ink is thy blood

You need to allow yourself to bleed.

Carlie sat on her bed toying with a pen and glaring at an open notebook, the blank page mocking her. She considered the words of her boyfriend for the umpteenth time and it did nothing more than make her feel upset. She knew he was right—shallow, unbelievable characters had long been a point of contention with her beta readers—but it still stung to hear it.

She tossed the pen aside and grabbed a book of prompts she bought earlier but nothing inspired her. Ideas and notions glimmered in the far distance of her mind, like the fireflies of her youth that blinked and teased her into chasing them only to end with darkness and the dissatisfaction of tiny fists that turned up empty when unclenched.

Then: inspiration. Carlie picked up a safety pin from her nightstand and examined it. Silver and shiny, with a sharp tip. She held it carefully in her left hand and poked the tip of her right forefinger, gasping at the quick shock of pain. She jabbed it again and a drop of blood welled up. She grabbed her notebook, brought her finger to the paper. She tried to write the letter T but the blood smeared and streaked before she could cross it. She squeezed her fingertip again and got just enough to finish the job.

This wasn't what he meant by spilling your blood.

As she put the safety pin back on the nightstand she caught a glimpse of the scars on her left wrist. She glided her fingers over the raised lines. The voice in her head spoke softly with condescension—*you did it wrong. You couldn't even kill yourself the right way.*

Blood began to leak through the scars. She watched, mesmerized, as they formed four neat little lines of blood across both her wrists. Another voice rose from the depths of her mind—*she'll be fine. The cuts are shallow and she didn't cut in the right direction.* She knew the voice well enough; it was Mrs. McIntyre, the school nurse using her best snooty soprano tone to explain to Carlie's panicked parents that their precious little mental patient was going to be just fine, but that maybe a psychiatrist and a plentiful diet of antidepressants should make the rest of her high school existence bearable. She seethed at the thought of the old bitch.

Her wrists began to ache and she felt like there were lots of little somethings crawling on her arms. She held her arms up in front of her and gasped. Rivulets of blood flowed down her arms in strange patterns, curling and twirling to form a cursive script that she couldn't quite make out.

It was when she shifted on the bed and felt dampness on her chest and her legs that she started freaking out. She pulled off her nightgown and ran to the full length mirror in the corner. Her eyes widened, horrified at the sight.

Every scar was bleeding.

The blood from her wrists told stories of low self-esteem and relentless bullying. The scars on her knees lamented of pain and failure. But the biggest story to be told came from the thrice-opened scar on her sternum. The crimson script read of vulnerability and weakness, vanity and uncertainty. But despite all this, there were still words of hope and survival.

"Carlie?"

Mike stood at the bedroom door, mouth agape.

She turned to face him, her arms spread at her sides, the palms of her hands facing up.

"You want me to bleed on the page?" she said.

"Read this."

graveyard of broken hearts

Angie's here—it must be Valentine's Day. She parks three rows away from me by a rusted garbage can. She walks slowly in her funereal best, topped off by a veiled pillbox hat. She clutches a handkerchief the way most old ladies would their pearls.

Every February 14th she's here begging forgiveness. This year there's a layer of anger in her sadness, a crispy edge to her tone.

"I saw your wife yesterday," she says. "I followed her around town. She seems less heartbroken these days. I don't understand how she could move on and I..." She's reaching hysteria faster than usual. She glares at my tombstone—more specifically, at the side where my wife's name is etched. Fury emanates off her as she kicks the glass candleholder and sends it crashing against the stone, where it lands at an awkward angle.

I rise from my resting place and stand before her.

"You never meant anything to me." She can't hear me, but her eyes widen as she feels the breeze from my words.

"Tony, is that you?" Her voice, full of hope and fear.

I reach out, watching as my hand sinks below the surface of her flesh, past blood and bone until I find her heart and squeeze it. Her hands rise to her chest, her face contorts. She struggles to breathe before she collapses against the gravestone behind her.

storage: empty

"Smile, beautiful!"

Mia gritted her teeth behind tightly sealed lips. She smiled, knowing the pictures would come out horrible. Kurt would disagree. He always did.

He snapped several pictures of her sitting on the couch. She hadn't been doing anything of note; she had planted herself on the middle of the sofa after breakfast, flipping back and forth between a rom-com and a heavily edited R-rated thriller.

She grabbed a tortilla chip and dunked it into a jar of cold queso. She held it up and made an O with her mouth, as if she were shocked about something. She popped the chip in her mouth and laughed as she tried unsuccessfully to lick a spot of queso that was just outside the corner of her lip.

"God, you're beautiful," he said as he snapped one last pic. His smile disappeared as he studied his phone.

"Geez, am I that ugly?"

"My phone storage is almost full." He wiped the remaining bit of cheese off her face and popped his finger in his mouth. "And you're not ugly at all. I've never seen a more beautiful woman than you."

"What? Come on."

"Nope. Just you."

"What about Sophia Loren?"

"Nope."

"Audrey Hepburn?"

"Nope."

"I've been sitting here like a slug all day eating chips and queso. I've gained at least thirty pounds since we moved into this place. How can you call me beautiful?"

Kurt kissed Mia on top of her head. "Because you are. So there."

"Your phone is full of pictures of me, is it?" He smiled in response.

"Maybe." He kissed the top of her head again. "I need to clean out my car so we can start packing for the trip. I'll be back in a few."

After he left, she grabbed his phone and went into his camera roll. He wasn't kidding—the majority of the pictures had her in them.

And she found fault with every single one of them.

The set of last ones he took—she looked like a mess, with her hair in an askew bun and wearing a pair of sweatpants that were once baggy. Her eyes were puffy and her cheeks reminded her of a squirrel that had stuffed its face with as much seed as possible. And that last one where she had the cheese stuck on her face? Her eyelids were half shut and she looked stoned.

Without hesitation, she deleted that picture. And then the one before that, and the one before that.

Delete.

Delete.

Delete.

As each memory disappeared, she felt lighter, giddier. The photos weren't all her; she left the memes and the shots of the mountain range from their last camping trip.

She stopped at a photo he took of her in Mystic when they were walking on a pier after dinner. She had a fondness for the dress she wore that night—sleeveless green lace, fitted on top and flared at the waist. The more she stared at it, the more flaws she found: her hair that she could never style perfectly, her crooked teeth, and her nose that she felt she never grew into.

Delete.

She kept going, so involved until she heard Kurt's question, confusion in his voice.

"What are you doing?" She never heard him come back in.

She held up his phone, which showed the first picture he took of her. It was from their third date, when he professed his love for her. They had gone to a café downtown and sat outside drinking coffee. When the rain came they dashed for cover under the awning. Soaked and freezing, they spoke those three words for the first time to each other and he took a selfie of them to keep the moment forever.

"I'm just taking care of your storage issue, darling." Mia hit the delete button one last time. The phone dropped to the floor as she disappeared.

divorce and roadkill

The bird was black and sleek with beady eyes and Emma wouldn't have known that about this particular bird had it not decided—seemingly on a whim—to commit suicide by dive bombing her car.

She was late for work as it was. Her windows were barely defrosted as she sped through the parking lot of her apartment complex. She screamed as the bird swooped in too low and crashed into her bumper. Emma glanced in the rearview mirror and saw a dark blur on the ground. A second longer look through the quickly defrosting rear windshield showed the bird on its side, one wing flapping wildly as if it thought it was still flying.

Emma turned the car off and began sobbing. With shaking hands, she opened the door and stepped out of the car. As she walked towards the bird she wondered what she was going to do with it. She didn't want to leave it in the road to get squashed by one of the neighbors, but she was apprehensive about touching it. She remembered that she had a beach towel in the trunk. She popped the lid and pulled the towel from a broken cardboard box. She walked over to the bird and got down on one knee beside it.

"Hey there," she said. She wasn't sure why she was talking to it—it wasn't going to answer her. "Why did you go flying in front of the car? Why my car?"

One of her neighbors slowed as they drove by her and gave her a curious look. She pretended to not see him and turned her attention back to the bird. It had stopped flapping that one wing and stared at her with those beady eyes, all black with the spark fading away.

Emma knew that look—Owen, her ex, had given her the same look when she told him that she was leaving. The day she came over for the last of her stuff there was no sign of life in his eyes. A couple of months later he wrapped his brand new Charger around the oldest oak tree in Harbinger Memorial Park. His blood alcohol content was ten times the limit.

He never would have driven in that condition. She wondered if he had stopped caring. In the end, leaving him was the right decision but there were days when it still hurt.

The bird cawed weakly at her. She folded the beach towel in half and in half again before placing it over the bird. Her hands still trembling, she tucked the towel ends underneath and carefully picked it up. The bird didn't put up a fight. She got back into her car, all the time being extra careful with her little package as she set it on the passenger seat. It lay there wrapped up in its colorful towel, any sign of life close to gone.

She stroked the bird gently through the towel and felt a tiny shudder. She picked him up—she decided that the bird was a he—and held him close to her chest with the hopes that her heartbeat would inspire his fading one to continue on.

It didn't work. He stared at her with dead black eyes.

"I'm sorry," Emma whispered. Her throat tightened up as the tears began to fall again. She placed him gingerly in her lap and started the car. At the end of the driveway, she turned right instead of the usual left to get to the highway. She wasn't sure where she was going and she didn't really care. After a few turns and waits at traffic lights she found herself at Harbinger Memorial Park.

She never drove down this way, not even after Owen's accident. She didn't attend the services; it had been made clear that she was not welcome, so she spent that evening curled up under her comforter with a bottle of merlot and an overwhelming sense of guilt.

If she hadn't left, he would most likely still be among the living. If she had stayed, it was anyone's guess how much time it would have been before she ended up in the final unfortunate position Owen chose for himself.

To call Harbinger Memorial a park was a stretch, to be sure. It was more like a triangular island of green between a few intersections that someone in town thought would be a great place to put in a swing set and a slide. There was no parking lot, just a few parallel spots on one of the three surrounding streets. She parked at the far end of Hawthorne Street and held the bird tight to her as she walked through the grass.

Finding the tree was an easy enough job: the crime scene tape was long gone but the tree still stood. There was a small wooden cross and a bouquet of flowers at the base of the oak. *Forever in our hearts,* the inscription on the cross read. The tears started again, spilling hot down her cheeks and dripping onto the bird.

"I didn't mean to hurt you."

She placed the bird, still wrapped in the towel, next to the cross. For a moment she stood there awkwardly—should she say a prayer? Have a moment of silence? She was far from the religious sort, so she stood there for another minute, staring at the bird and the cross.

The bird dying wasn't her fault. She wanted to think that in time, she would feel the same way about Owen.

"I'm sorry," she whispered.

She walked away from the tree. As she pressed the button to unlock her car she saw a box truck coming around the corner too fast and too close to her side of the road.

The guilt can stop. You know what to do.

Emma stepped into the street, in front of her car. Two more steps would end everything.

The truck kept speeding. She took a deep breath. Closed her eyes. She stepped forward once, hesitant about the next one.

The truck blew by and the rush of wind accompanying it made her stagger. She ran her fingers through her hair as she squinted in the wake of debris kicked up by the truck. She got in the car and popped a CD in. The voice of Glen Phillips filled the car as he sang of grief and praise and love and loss and moving on. Emma drove away and sang along, her voice growing stronger with each song.

the new me

(life affirmation)

late at night

I emerge from my chrysalis

to examine

the new world

around me

with new wings I soar

above hills and over trees

near the lake I see

strings of lights

calling

calling

calling me

but I ignore the lights

and move on

I come back

to a place I once knew

and find those I loved

are gone

the mirror beckons me

and again we lock eyes

this time

I recognize her:

she with the haunted eyes

from the ghosts who broke free

she who hid behind her hair

to keep everyone away

she smiles at me

and I smile back

as I say:

I've been knocked down

and yet I rise

and continue to survive.

about the author

doungjai gam's short fiction has appeared in *Tough, LampLight, Distant Dying Ember, Now I Lay Me Down To Sleep,* and *Wicked Haunted.* she was a sixteen-time winner in the Necon E-Books Flash Fiction contests and has appeared in the Necon E-Books *Best of Flash Fiction Anthology* series from 2011 on. she is a member of the New England Horror Writers. Born in Thailand, she currently resides in Connecticut with author Ed Kurtz and their little black cat Oona. in her downtime she enjoys road trips, lattes, and playing Pearl Jam on repeat.

you can find gam on:
    facebook @doungjaigambooks
    twitter: @djai76
    instagram: @djai76

acknowledgements

first and foremost, endless thanks to Jacob Haddon and Apokrupha Press for their guidance, support and (most of all!!) patience over the last three years as I slowly put this collection together. life has a tendency to get in the way and mess things up and I'm grateful to Jacob for his understanding. also, many thanks to Robert Ford for the amazing cover—I love it!

to my parents, family, and friends who have supported me along the way and encouraged me to keep following this dream of mine—all my love to you.

thank you to those who have previously published some of these little stories over the last few years: Jacob Haddon, Tim Deal, Russ Thompson at Hellnotes, and the members of the team who judged the Necon flash fiction contests.

and speaking of Necon...shoutout to my second family! thank you for making me feel like I belong, even though I always feel like I am on the outside peeking in.

much thanks to PD Cacek, Brian Hodge, Jim Moore, Tony Tremblay, Bracken MacLeod, and Ed Kurtz for their love, friendship, and advice over the years.

thanks to my beta readers for pointing out when things don't seem right...and for understanding when I don't always listen. (I do listen sometimes, don't get me wrong) to EKZ and Oona...forever, my loves.

and finally: to my writing mentor and Beta Reader #1, Thomas Tessier...none of this would have been possible if you hadn't taken a chance on me all those years ago. all my thanks, love, and gratitude to you. I hope I've done you proud.

oh, and while I'm thinking about it, this is the music I wrote this book to: Pearl Jam, Jeff Buckley, The Verve, Travis, Starsailor, Coldplay, Toad the Wet Sprocket and Glen Phillips, Tori Amos, and Keane. I name check a few songs in the story notes if you're looking for a soundtrack for this.

story credits

(some have been edited/revised from their previous publication)

Necon E-Books Flash Fiction Anthology Best of 2011 (eds. Bob Booth and Matt Bechtel, Necon E-Book Press)

- I'll make you famous

Necon E-Books Flash Fiction Anthology Best of 2013 (eds. Bob Booth and Matt Bechtel, Necon E-Book Press)

- best served warm
- huntress
- lake of secrets
- repose

Necon E-Books Flash Fiction Anthology Best of 2014 (forthcoming)

- the key is the key
- rebirth
- the eater of dreams
- mama's wrath
- evening theft

Necon E-Books Flash Fiction Anthology Best of 2015 (forthcoming)

- the south rises again
- love.lust.obesssion.whatever.
- in his dreams (for Dave)
- one day we will dance again
- waste not, want not

Hellnotes.com "Horror in a Hundred" series (Russ Thompson, hellnotes.com, 2014)

- light box
- beware of darkness
- bloodrain

LampLight Magazine, volume 2, issue 3:

- what remains

Anthology Year Three: Distant Dying Ember (Tim Deal, The Four Horsemen LLC, 2015)

- how you killed me

selected story notes

I'll make you famous: this was my first Necon E-Books flash fiction contest win. the rules that month were to write a story using words from a list selected by the judges. my writing mentor Tom Tessier suggested a direction to take, but he thought I should remove the line about "Pam or Sam Something." I had thrown it in as a self-referential joke (almost nobody gets my name right on the first try). I realize how much this sounds like a "don't listen to your mentor" statement, but it's not. absolutely listen and take their words to heart, but also don't be afraid to speak up if you disagree. a little debate doesn't hurt.

best served warm: another Necon flash winner, and the shortest piece in the collection. the theme that month was food. I knew I had wanted to do something with peanut allergies (even going as far as asking a friend what it felt like when the allergic reaction kicked in), but in the end decided to have it read kind of like recipe directions. of the pieces I've written to date, this is one of my favorites.

lake of secrets: the inspiration for this one came from the Fuel song "Hemmorhage (In My Hands)." I thought I misheard the line "drag the waters till the depths give up their dead" while driving to work one morning and I grabbed my scratchpad and jotted a couple of lines down. yes, while I was driving. no, I don't recommend it. trying to decipher what I wrote afterwards not as much fun as one might think it is.

love. lust. obsession. whatever.: most of the flash pieces I've written took a week or two, but not the case with this one. it came in a burst and with revisions it took about half an hour, but I was never fond of the last line (This pain will never compare to what you put me though). when my editor Jacob Haddon sent me revision notes, his suggestion was to revise that last line and somehow tie it back to the fairy tale glass slipper bit from the beginning of the story. I'm a lot happier now with the ending.

evening theft: the title is a play on the Jeff Buckley song Morning Theft. a few days after his body was found in 1996, I had a dream where I was talking to him on the phone and suddenly there were weird noises and colors and I woke up to Last Goodbye blaring loudly. but *Grace* was in its CD case and the radio wasn't on.

christmas lights in february: I was driving to a writers' group meeting and maybe going a bit fast down some back roads, blasting *Grace* by Jeff Buckley and in tears for no particular reason. I remember seeing Christmas lights and thinking that people needed to take that shit down because the holidays were over. out of that sadness came this.

one day we will dance again: I had this vision of a couple sharing ear buds, holding each other in the moonlight and swaying gently. what were they listening to? my guess would be One Day by The Verve (in time, I also guessed maybe Sirens by Pearl Jam).

torn: in the movie *Smoke Signals*, Arlene Joseph (played by the wonderful Tantoo Cardinal) says to her son Victor how she feels like she's literally in pieces after her husband left them. this story came to be between that scene and my obsessive listening to of the song Torn by Ednaswap (most people know that song courtesy of Natalie Imbruglia). their version can be found on YouTube—if you can find Ednaswap singer Anne Previn's version from the Howard Stern show, even better.

rebirth: this one is about our friend the dandelion. I know people tend to look down on them, but these guys provide food for the bees and give little pops of color on your lawns.

mama's wrath: for this one, I thought of Mother Nature getting pissed off at the tourists who go on vacation to beautiful beaches and then destroy the environment with their disgusting littering habits.

in his dreams…: when my brother-in-law Dave passed away, to say that there was a lot of anger and sadness going around would be an understatement. my hope for him is that wherever he is now, it's beautiful and quiet and peaceful.

footsteps.: this one...I struggled about putting this in here or leaving it out. When my brother died, I felt like my life was in slow motion. it took me a week and a half before I had an appetite. it took me a couple of months before I could get back into reading again, and I'm still struggling with that. most of the books I was reading at the time I still have not been able to pick up over two years later. but writing...that was what kept me going. this was the first piece I wrote after he died, and I read it at his service. I only added the last four words recently.

bloodrain: inspired strongly by Tori Amos's cover of Raining Blood by Slayer; or rather, the imagery she had of a vulva raining blood down on abusive men.

reflection: because some days you look at yourself in the mirror and have no idea who is staring back at you. sometimes it's a physical thing, but other times you look into your own eyes and see nothing and that's fucking terrifying.

the dying house: I'm not sure how the phrase "the ghost behind her eyes" got into my head, but I do know this piece was written after the death of my brother so I'm sure it evolved from those events. as I alluded to in the story notes for footsteps., the one thing that sustained me in those first few months was a steady diet of journals and pens, words flowing. lunch breaks, weekends, late nights—I couldn't stop. I wish every day that the circumstances for that burst had never happened.

that girl with the hair: anyone who has spent a significant amount of time with me will tell you I like to hide behind my hair—hell, my dad would jokingly call me Veronica Lake. I thought it would be neat to write a story about someone who was hiding something in her hair.

some animals eat their young: if you've read the short story "The Rifle" from *Peaceable Kingdom* by the late Jack Ketchum (and if you haven't, you should remedy that) then you might see where the inspiration for this came from. Dallas Mayr (how many of us knew Ketchum) was an amazing writer who loved cats and Dewar's and was willing to help out up and coming writers. I wasn't close to him, but he was an inspiration and influence to me. my favorite memory I have of him is from Necon 32, where we chatted as he signed some books for me. I showed him a copy of I'll make you famous. He read it, chuckled, and said he liked it.

cold: this is easily the oldest story in here, dating back to 1996. The inspiration for this one came from Walk On The Ocean by Toad The Wet Sprocket and In Hiding by Pearl Jam, but mostly the former. this is one of those stories that I play with every few years but couldn't really get it right, so back into the folder it went. I like to think now that I finally got it right.

timekeeper: I met my friend Tommy in 2010 when he joined my ex-husband's band as the lead singer. previously he had drummed in several bands in the local CT metal scene over the years, and though he sang lead, he still drummed for other bands. I used to joke with him that he was in like thirty bands at a time. I kinda wish that I had the chops for rhyming poetry and had written this in a way that it could be smooth with a drum beat.

how you killed me.: this one took a few tries before I found it a home with Tim Deal and the anthology that was put out every year by the late and much missed AnthoCon held in New Hampshire from 2011-2015. part of the inspiration came from "Heartsick," a short story from Brian Hodge's amazing collection The Convulsion Factory (haven't read him? fix that right now!).

what remains: my first sale, bought by Jacob Haddon for LampLight magazine in 2014. this story was the result of a nightmare that woke me up in a panic, convinced that someone was in the shadows. I'd hear stairs creaking, but in the end my cat Lily hopped on the bed and startled the crap out of me.

thy ink is thy blood: my partner Ed and I have different writing styles, and he told me one day that he feared bleeding on the pages at the level I do. I told him he shouldn't be. I find it cathartic but it doesn't necessarily mean that every word or every story written on the page needs to see the light of day.

storage: empty: this came in a low self-esteem burst of anger. I wondered what it would be like to delete all your pictures of yourself. would you disappear? sometimes I've had that hope. I think at some point or another we have all had that thought about disappearing.

divorce and roadkill: the incident with the bird happened to me, but it was rush hour at a very busy intersection and it was impossible to stop and assist the bird. the image of the poor creature in my rearview mirror on the ground with one wing still flapping still haunts me. at the time this happened, I was separated and living on my own for the first time. a lot of pent-up feelings were let out in many tears. some people didn't understand—I was told the bird was waving goodbye to me and that I shouldn't have been so upset and that I was strong enough to deal with this. that poor little blackbird was a sum of everything hitting me at once—seven deaths in the span of fourteen months, my separation and eventual divorce, years of depression and anxiety, and the realization that I was an incredibly broken person.

the new me: and when I realized I was broken, I chose to heal myself.

LampLight Volume 2

lamplightmagazine.com/volume-2

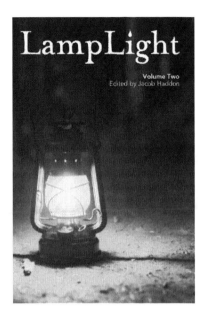

This second annual anthology from LampLight Magazine collects the four great issues from September 2013 to June 2014

Includes the complete novella, The Devoted, featuring Jonathan Crowley, by James A Moore.

Fiction and interviews from our featured writers: Norman Prentiss, Kealan Patrick Burke, Mary SanGiovanni and Holly Newstein.

J.F. Gonzalez continues his history of the genre in his Shadows in the Attic series. LampLight Classics brings you some great classic stories.

Fiction by: Michael Knost, Christopher Bleakley, Emma Whitehall, David Tallerman, M. R. Jordan, Lauren Forry, Dave Thomas, Arinn Dembo, Bracken MacLeod, doungjai gam, Tim W Boiteau, Alethea Eason, Lucy A Snyder, Colleen Jurkiewicz, Curtis James McConnell, Victor Cypert, Catherine Grant

Made in the USA
Middletown, DE
05 January 2019